For Peter and Laura ~
I will love you forever
~ ASC

For the dear friends who became parents as I worked on this book:
JB & AB, SAC & SC, KED & DG, ME & ED, DF & JW,
JF & EF, JUH & AH, SP & YK, KKS & AS.
~ LA

Text copyright © 2017 by Alyssa Satin Capucilli · Illustrations copyright © 2017 by Lisa Anchin · All rights reserved. Published by Orchard Books, an imprint of Scholastic Inc., *Publishers since 1920*. ORCHARD BOOKS and design are registered trademarks of Watts Publishing Group, Ltd., used under license. SCHOLASTIC and associated logos are trademarks and/or registered trademarks of Scholastic Inc. · The publisher does not have any control over and does not assume any responsibility for author or third-party websites or their content. · No part of this publication may be reproduced, stored in a retrieval system, or transmitted in any form or by any means, electronic, mechanical, photocopying, recording, or otherwise, without written permission of the publisher. For information regarding permission, write to Scholastic Inc., Attention: Permissions Department, 557 Broadway, New York, NY 10012. · This book is a work of fiction. Names, characters, places, and incidents are either the product of the author's imagination or are used fictitiously, and any resemblance to actual persons, living or dead, business establishments, events, or locales is entirely coincidental. · Library of Congress Cataloging-in-Publication Data Available · ISBN 978-0-545-80310-6
10 9 8 7 6 5 4 3 2 1   17 18 19 20 21 · Printed in China   62 · First edition, April 2017 · The text type was set in Delius and Delius Swash Caps. · The display type was hand-lettered. Book design by Doan Buu

I will love you

By
Alyssa Satin Capucilli

Illustrated by
Lisa Anchin

Orchard Books
New York · An Imprint of Scholastic Inc.

In the very first moment,
  when you came to be,
I looked at you,
  and you looked at me . . .

The sun shined *hello,*
    and the moon winked, too.
And clouds bounced by
    filled with dreams, just for you.

Then nuzzled in a blanket of stars from the sky,
With the twinkling lights singing a sweet lullaby,

I whispered these words as I held you near,

For all time, for all space, for the world to hear . . .

I will love you as sure
      as the breeze loves the flowers,

And as long as smooth stones talk

of hours and hours.

As you're soothed by the hush of a butterfly's wings,

Or tickled by the rainbow a silky rain brings.

I will love you like the velvet-green hill loves its trees,
Like warm, misty shadows calling,
"Nestle with me."

With each dandelion wish that soars to the sky . . .
With each seed that blossoms over low, over high . . .

When the sea asks you, "Why?"
When you ask the sands, "When?"

When you wonder, and wander,
Far-and-wide-over-again.

When the world shares its smiles,
And sometimes its blues . . .

When the gift of *just being* . . .

wraps snugly 'round you . . .

And if you should call out . . .
I'll call back, "Here I am."
I will be with you always . . .
wherever I am.

When the lark wakes the butter-yellow dawn in its flight . . .
When the fireflies dance, *good night, good night . . .*

When you reach for this whisper of words in your ear . . .
For all time, for all space, for forever. *Everywhere . . .*